# ECO RANGERS

## MICROBAT MAYHEM

*For Dimity.*

NEW FRONTIER PUBLISHING

American edition published in 2021
by New Frontier Publishing USA,
an imprint of New Frontier Publishing Europe Ltd.
www.newfrontierpublishing.us

First published in the UK in 2019
by New Frontier Publishing Europe Ltd
Uncommon, 126 New King's Rd, Fulham, London SW6 4LZ
www.newfrontierpublishing.co.uk

ISBN: 978-1-913639-07-5

Illustrated by Aśka, www.askaillustration.com
Text copyright © 2019, 2021 Candice Lemon-Scott
Illustrations copyright © 2019, 2021 New Frontier Publishing
The moral right of the author has been asserted.

Distributed in the United States and Canada by Lerner Publishing Group Inc
241 First Avenue North, Minneapolis, MN 55401 USA
www.lernerbooks.com

Library of Congress Catalogue-in-Publication Data Available

Edited by Stephanie Stahl
Designed by Rachel Lawston

Printed in China

FSC
www.fsc.org
MIX
From responsible
sources
FSC® C130668

1 3 5 7 9 10 8 6 4 2

# ECO RANGERS
## MICROBAT MAYHEM

# CANDICE LEMON-SCOTT

## Illustrated by Aśka

## MEET THE ECO RANGERS

# EBONY

Hi everyone, I'm Ebony! I'm twelve years old. I like spending time in nature, rescuing animals or riding my bike to go off on an adventure. I'm super independent, but sometimes I jump right in without thinking and that can get me into trouble! I love being an Eco Ranger because I get to solve mysteries!

# JAY

I'm Jay, Ebony's best friend and next-door neighbor. I'm eleven years old. I like making jokes and have a bit of a sweet tooth… especially when it comes to cake! I also love nature and helping out at the wildlife hospital. Being an Eco Ranger is so much fun because I can look after animals and make sure they are safe.

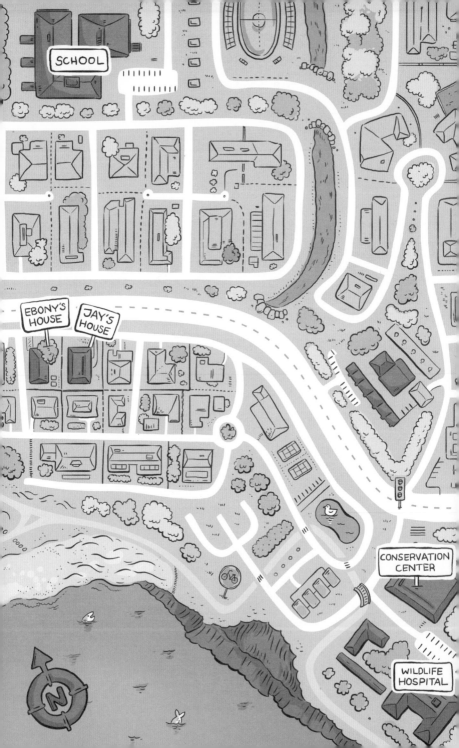

"One more ride?" Ebony pleaded.

Ebony and Jay had only an hour left at Super World theme park before it closed. The two Eco Rangers had spent all their free time caring for sick and injured wildlife, so the conservation center had given them an annual pass to the park as a thank you.

Jay grimaced, pulling his cap down over his face, as though it would make him disappear. He hated scary rides, but Ebony loved them. She pulled her unruly brown hair back in a ponytail and dragged him toward the Wild Jungle ride. It took passengers through dark tunnels and caves with mechanical animals like snakes and giant spiders, and jets of water spraying out.

"Come on! We wouldn't be the Eco Rangers if we didn't go on the Wild Jungle ride," Ebony said.

"Okay, just once," Jay sighed. "I'm only going on it because you're my best friend, but I'm not sitting at the front!" Ebony winked at him, delighted.

When they got to the ride she was disappointed to see it was closed. A gray steel fence was up around it and a big billboard on the front read, "Nightmare Flyer. Coming Soon." Next to that sign was a smaller one on the gate, "Demolition Site. DO NOT ENTER."

"Oh no! They've closed down the jungle ride," Ebony said. "The new one will be cool though, I guess."

"No way, it sounds terrifying! Do you want to get an ice cream before we go home?"

Jay asked as he leaned against the gate.

Ebony didn't have time to answer. Suddenly the gate swung open and Jay fell flat on his face.

"Ouch!" he mumbled into the ground.

He pulled himself to his feet, his face and glasses covered in dirt.

Ebony laughed. "I guess the gate is now open!"

"Um, the sign says, 'DO NOT ENTER.'"

Ebony stepped past Jay, ignoring him.

"This will only get us in trouble, Ebony." Jay wiped his glasses with his favorite Eco Ranger T-shirt and reluctantly followed her in.

Ebony scrambled over tufts of overgrown grass and some scraps of metal lying around the old ride. She could see the dark, empty entrance. There were artificial hollows and trees around it. It was spooky seeing the ride closed. As she reached a painted hollow, she heard a *tick-tick-tick* sound coming from the base of it. She stepped closer and heard the noise again. At that moment, Jay tapped her on the shoulder. She jumped in fright.

"We shouldn't be in here. It's giving me the creeps," Jay said.

"There's something near the hollow," Ebony cried.

Jay pushed his glasses against his nose and squinted.

"I can't see anything," he said.

"No, but listen, I can hear it." Ebony bent down, following the noise. She pushed blades of grass aside gently, revealing two tiny creatures. "Look at this!" she gasped.

They were dark brown and hairless and no bigger than her thumb. They each had small leathery wings covering their bodies and a tiny furry head. *Bats!* But they weren't like the long-eared bats Ebony saw around her house. They were much smaller.

"What are they?" Jay asked, crouching down next to her.

Their tiny wings moved slightly as they made that chattering sound.

"Baby bats!" she cried. "And they're still alive."

"What should we do with them?" Jay asked.

Ebony looked at the animals. They were so fragile. Leaving them for even a moment might be too late for them. She didn't know how long they'd already been without their mom. Their little tummies were sunken. Their wings looked dry, like paper that could tear easily.

"Quick!" She pulled Jay's cap off his head, placing it in his hands. "We'll use this."

"Hey, that cap's special. I won it at the football finals last year," he cried.

"Please, it's for the baby bats," Ebony smiled, and Jay nodded grudgingly. "Just hold it still."

The cap would be perfect for carrying them back. Now she needed something to pick the bats up with. The Eco Rangers had recently gone to a special wildlife talk. They knew never to touch a bat or any wildlife animal with their bare hands in case they were scratched or bitten. But what could she use to scoop them up? It had to be small and soft.

"I know!" Ebony said. She ripped off her right shoe and pulled off her sock.

"Pyewww! You're going to kill them with the smell," Jay exclaimed.

"My feet do not smell." Ebony sniffed her sock and screwed up her nose. "Well, not much anyway. It's the best we've got."

She placed the sock over her hand like a mitten and looked at the tiny bats. Their little black eyes opened as though they knew the Eco Rangers were there to rescue them. She then very carefully placed her gloved hand over one of the bats, scooped it up and gently released it into the cap. She did the same with the other bat. One of the bats stretched out its wings, then bent them back in again. It was like it was wrapping itself in a blanket. The other one shook a little, then they huddled in close like they were keeping each other warm.

"They're probably cold," Jay said, peering into the cap.

"They don't look very well," Ebony agreed.

"There are these little eggs on the bats too. Eww!" Jay said, scrunching his nose.

They had to get them the help they needed, and quickly. But it was late. The wildlife hospital would be closing soon. Ebony got out her phone and sent an emergency message to the vets, Doctor Bat and Doctor Tan.

"I hope we can get them to the hospital in time to save them," she said.

"Me too," Jay agreed.

The Eco Rangers had stayed out past
their curfew so they quickly cycled home.
Hopefully they would not get into too
much trouble with their parents! Jay
pedaled extra carefully, with his cap holding
the bats in his bike crate. Ebony dropped
her bike on the front lawn. Jay leaned his
against the front of her house and carried
the bats inside.

"Mom, you'll never believe what we
found," Ebony began, holding Jay's cap out
toward her.

"You're home late," Ebony's mom said.

"I was getting worried."

"I'm sorry, Mom, but we found something at the theme park. Look!" Ebony said.

Ebony's mom looked at the tiny bats. "Argh!" she screamed. "What are those things?"

"They're baby bats," Ebony said.

"Could you take us to the conservation center? We need to get them to the wildlife hospital as soon as possible." Jay added in his politest voice, "Please?"

Ebony's mom frowned. "It's late on a Saturday. The center will be closed by now for the rest of the weekend."

"We have special Eco Ranger privileges and I already sent them an emergency alert," Ebony said. "The vets just texted me back now to say they can meet us there."

"Okay, okay," Ebony's mom said.

"Thanks, you're the best," Jay smiled.

One of the hospital vets was already waiting by the front doors of the conservation center when they arrived. Ebony giggled when she saw it was Doctor Bat, who was there to greet them. Even though Doctor Battacharjee was her full name, everyone called her Doctor Bat for short. Soon, Doctor Bat would meet two baby bats!

"Hi, Eco Rangers!" She nodded at the kids. She turned to Ebony's mom, then looked around as though searching for someone else. "What's the emergency? I was expecting to see a wildlife friend that needed our help."

The vet tucked a strand of straggly gray hair behind her ear, the wrinkles on her forehead deepening.

"They're in here," Ebony said, holding up Jay's cap.

Doctor Bat raised an eyebrow. "They?"

"Yeah," Jay said. "Ebony found baby bats at Super World theme park."

"Two of them," Ebony's mom added.

Doctor Bat grinned. "Is this a joke? Are you making fun of my name?"

"Did someone say fun?" It was Doctor Tan, the other vet at the center. He leaned down to look.

Ebony quickly explained what had happened and lifted the cap to show them the baby bats. Doctor Tan looked down his long nose at them.

"They're tiny," Doctor Tan said. "Hmmm, dehydrated. Lice present."

"Lice? And they're in my cap?" Jay screeched. "That's just great!"

"Let me look." Doctor Bat peered inside Jay's cap and examined the baby bats closely. "These are microbats to be exact. Hmmm, one female, one male."

"Will they survive?" Ebony's mom asked.

"They're very young," Doctor Bat said. "These microbats are less than three weeks old, I'd say, since they're still hairless.

They must have fallen from their mom. Sadly, it happens sometimes. They'll need special care until they can be returned to their home."

"Where did you say you found them?" Doctor Tan asked.

Ebony turned red as she explained how she went into the old Wild Jungle ride site.

"Ebony!" her mom cried.

"I don't need to tell you about the danger of going into a ride that's about to be demolished." Doctor Bat frowned. "And about handling bats. You should *never* pick one up with your hands."

"Yes, I remembered so I used one of my socks," Ebony said sheepishly.

"It's rare in microbats, but they can have lyssavirus. It's a very dangerous disease if people get it. That's why you were vaccinated when you first became the Eco Rangers."

"How could we forget?" Jay shivered.

Ebony remembered he had nearly fainted

when he got the injection.

"We'll keep the little bats here for observation overnight and give them a lice treatment. And, if you want to keep that cap, Jay, we'll need to give that a good clean too!"

Jay paled. Ebony wasn't sure if it was at the thought of the needle he'd had or because his special cap now had lice. She did feel a teeny bit guilty about using it for the bats.

"Now it's time for these babies to get their injections. Let's get them rehydrated."

They all followed Doctor Bat inside the hospital and down to one of the medical rooms, the vet carrying the bats carefully in Jay's cap. Doctor Tan shuffled around in drawers, getting out the items they'd need.

"This is a special fluid to hydrate them," Doctor Tan explained. Then he gave each of the baby bats an injection.

"What are you going to call them?"

Doctor Tan asked.

"Batman and Robin," Jay said.

Ebony laughed. "But one's a girl!"

"Robin can be a girl's name," Jay said. "With a Y."

"True." Ebony couldn't argue with that. "Batman and Robyn it is!"

Doctor Tan smiled and placed the bats carefully inside a pouch, not much different to Ebony's sock, only not stinky!

"Where do you think the bats' mom is?" Ebony asked.

"She's most likely back with her colony. Sometimes microbat moms give birth in what's called a maternity cave," Doctor Bat said.

"A what?" Jay asked.

"It's a special spot they go to for having their babies. It can be a hollow in a tree, a drain, a cave, anywhere dark and quiet. They stay in there during the day and then come out at night to feed."

"Wow!" Ebony said. "You don't think the bat colony is inside the Wild Jungle ride, do you?"

"I'm sure the site would have been checked before they closed it down for demolition," Doctor Bat continued. "The mom could have come out from a hollow or other dark place to feed on insects. She might have fallen and got hurt, so she couldn't make her way back. We can try and find the bats' family when they're ready for release. Right now, the only thing we need to worry about is making these babies grow nice, strong, and healthy."

Ebony nodded, but she had this strange feeling there might be more to worry about than the orphaned microbats.

Ebony's mom brought the Eco Rangers back to the conservation center early on Sunday morning. Ebony shook with excitement to see the baby bats had made it through the night and were doing well.

The Eco Rangers had stayed up late last night getting a small portable bat home ready. Jay's mom had quickly sewed two pouches from an old baby blanket, while Ebony used a container without its lid to keep the pouched babies in, so they couldn't escape. Jay showed the vets the bat home proudly.

"Great job, Eco Rangers!" Doctor Tan said. "Now, it's time for Operation Bat Babysitting." Doctor Tan brought out two pairs of special gloves for the Eco Rangers to wear while holding the bats. As they put them on, he got out two plastic syringes to feed Batman and Robyn, one for each of the bats, and filled them with a milky formula.

"This is just like their mom's milk," said Doctor Tan. "Only give them this, warmed up. No other type of milk. It's got some other goodies in it too, to help make them nice and strong."

Doctor Bat showed the Eco Rangers how to hold the bats upright for feeding. Ebony and Jay took one each.

"Careful with their wings," Doctor Bat said. "Okay, now gently place the syringe tip in front of the bat's mouth."

Doctor Tan handed Jay and Ebony a syringe each. Ebony put hers to Robyn's tiny face. She opened her mouth wide and hungrily fed from the tiny syringe. The bat hung onto the edge of her finger with little claw-like hands at the end of her wings. Her little nostrils flared as she suckled, and her leathery ears were pulled back. She was the cutest little thing.

"Robyn sure is hungry," Ebony laughed.

"So is Batman," Jay grinned. "That's my kind of bat. He loves his food!"

The vets showed them how to tell when the bats were full.

"They should have slightly rounded bellies but no bigger than this," said Doctor Bat. "It's just as important not to let them get too full. They'll need to be fed every four hours to start with."

Next, Doctor Tan handed the Eco Rangers a cotton swab each.

"My ears are already clean," Jay said.

"They're not for your ears," Doctor Tan explained. "You need to give your bat's tummy a little rub and then, ah, do the same on the bat's bottom until it relieves itself."

"Eww, no way." Jay grimaced.

Ebony laughed.

"You need to do it for Robyn too." Ebony stopped laughing. "It's very important or the bats can get their waste stuck inside them and they could die."

Ebony did as she was instructed. She loved looking after wildlife, but some parts weren't as fun! Just as the vet said, it worked, and Robyn relieved herself on the cotton swab. Ebony quickly tossed it in the bin.

"This is disgusting," Jay said to Batman. "Lucky you're so cute."

Doctor Tan put the little bats back in their pouches.

"I've put a heating pad in each pouch. You'll need to keep them heated since the babies are too young to keep themselves warm without their mom," he explained.

Batman and Robyn were put inside their insect container crib, where they fell asleep.

"That's everything you need to know for now. They can stay in the container until they grow fur, when they'll be big enough to be released into an enclosure to learn to fly," Doctor Bat explained. "You can take them home with you now. Good Luck, Eco Rangers!"

The vets gave the two friends the bat care supplies to take home and waved them goodbye.

�

Back home, Ebony and Jay got the milk ready for the microbats' next feed. Ebony stared at the helpless babies, curled up together, their wings wrapped around themselves. She put on her special gloves and took Robyn from the container. She knew which was her bat because Robyn had slightly bigger ears than Batman and her eyes were closer together. They had the funniest little faces. The vets had explained their ears were so big and wide because they used sound to find their food. She gently took off the pouch that was keeping Robyn warm. She held her bat upright in the palm of her hand and Robyn gripped onto Ebony's hand with her little feet. The baby opened her mouth, revealing a set of small sharp teeth. She sucked down the milk hungrily.

"Check out Batman!" Jay laughed.

The baby bat was crawling up his arm, using his front claw to hook himself in and his back feet to climb up. Ebony was surprised by how fast he could move.

"Hey, that tickles," Jay laughed.

Once the bats had finished their milk, the Eco Rangers carefully put them in their cozy pouches and back in their container. Ebony smiled as they closed their black eyes and fell straight to sleep. As she looked at the bats, something still bothered her. What was going to happen to them once they were big enough to be released back into the wild, with no mom and without their colony? The colony had to be in that theme park somewhere, she was sure of it.

"Come on, Jay," she said. "We're going back to Super World."

"Seriously?" Jay groaned.

"Yes!" Ebony said firmly. "Microbats belong in colonies. The vets said it themselves. The babies we found wouldn't have gone too far from it. So, if Batman and Robyn are going to survive back in the wild, we need to find their bat family!"

That afternoon, the Eco Rangers put their bikes in the bike racks, scanned their theme park passes at the front entrance and headed toward the demolition site. As they walked up to it, they noticed a security guard coming in the opposite direction. Ebony gestured to Jay and they quickly hid behind a giant cartoon python cut-out.

The security guard grumbled into his radio, "Perimeter check complete. Heading up to Fairytale Castle now."

Ebony held her breath as she saw the guard's boots clomping past the cut-out they were hiding behind. When he'd walked past, she and Jay poked their heads out from behind the python. It was clear in both directions. They tiptoed out and went through the gate. It squeaked as Jay opened it. Ebony pressed her finger to her lips and Jay very slowly pulled it open the rest of the way and they went inside. Ebony gestured to the entrance of the Wild Jungle ride. Jay shivered.

"Come on, I bet the colony's in here!"

Ebony led Jay to the big dark entrance. She turned on the flashlight app on her phone, shining it on the ground. She could see the silvery tracks of the ride gleaming.

"Up here," she whispered.

They followed the tracks to the start of the ride, where the vehicles were. They sat empty, ghost-like now the Wild Jungle ride had closed down.

"Eww, I don't think it has been cleaned in a while," Jay said, making a face.

"Come on!" Ebony whispered.

She held out her phone flashlight and shone it around. The vehicles were imitation wooden canoes, so it looked like you were going down a jungle river when you went on the ride. The floor was painted in blue swirls to be the river. The walls were black and slick with pretend vines hanging down. Ebony stood right in the middle where the passengers used to board the ride. The empty tracks and vehicles were spooky. She felt cold, like a breeze had gone through the tunnel.

They had to go further in. Ebony took a deep breath, and the Eco Rangers walked carefully along the edge of the ride tracks until the tunnel opened out into a jungle cave. Ebony lifted the phone over her head so the light was shining on the roof.

"Whoa," she gasped, looking up.

Jay followed her gaze. The whole ceiling was covered in black moving objects. He screeched and jumped back, bashing into a passenger railing.

"Ouch!" he said, standing on one foot, as he clutched his ankle.

Ebony shone the flashlight a little closer. There were at least one hundred small bats no bigger than the palm of her hand. They covered the whole roof. They were hanging upside down, black leathery wings folded around them like a cocoon. Only their furry heads poked out. They were moving their wings out like they were doing a dance. Some flew around the domed ceiling. Ebony felt bat wings graze her face as a couple flew past her. She looked over at Jay. In the half-dark she could see him waving his arms about as the bats took flight, still standing on one foot.

"Wow, it's a whole colony all right!" Ebony said. "They must love it in here. It's dark and moist, and there's no one to disturb them."

"Yeah, but aren't they going to knock this ride down?" Jay said.

Ebony lowered the flashlight and the bats returned to their roosts, folding themselves in their winged blankets again. He was right. The bats would have to be moved before the ride was demolished. And where would they go? She switched to photo mode and took a picture of the bats.

"Let's go, we need to show this to the vets!"

She turned the flashlight back on and they followed the ride tracks, going back out the way they had come in. Soon they were blinded by the afternoon sun. Ebony turned off the flashlight and put her phone away. The Eco Rangers ran back through the tall grass. Finally, they reached the gate. As they swung it open, a dark shadow came over them.

"Hey! What are you kids doing in here?"

The Eco Rangers nearly bumped into the security guard from before. He hitched up his pants over his belly and glared at them grumpily, pulling on his ginger beard.

"N-n-nothing," Ebony stammered. "The gate was open. We thought—"

"You're old enough to read a sign, ain't ya? It says, do not enter."

"But we found a whole colony of bats in there. This ride can't be pulled down," Ebony said.

"I don't know nothing about no bats.

Get out of here, this is not a place for kids!"

"But—"

"Go!"

The Eco Rangers frowned and ran off, annoyed the guard wouldn't listen to them. *When the conservation center knew more bats were in here, they'd be sure to help rescue them*, Ebony thought.

❧

Ebony and Jay cycled straight to the conservation center. The vets greeted them with a smile.

"Hi, Eco Rangers. How are our bat superheroes doing?" Doctor Tan asked.

"They're really good," Ebony said.

"They drank all the milk you gave us already," Jay added.

"Oh, that's fine. I can get you some more," Doctor Tan laughed.

"We have a bigger problem," Ebony began. She quickly explained how they had sneaked back into the old ride and found the microbat colony.

"You really shouldn't have gone into that area again. It's not safe," Doctor Bat said.

"But I knew there had to be a colony nearby," Ebony said.

"And there was," Jay agreed.

"Are you sure it was bats you saw?" Doctor Tan said. Ebony showed the vets the photo of the bats she'd taken.

"This is a microbat colony." Doctor Tan sighed. "I wonder how they ended up in there."

"With so much of their natural habitat gone, animals like bats will look for anywhere dark and safe they can roost," Doctor Bat said.

"Yes, you're right, they probably settled in after the ride was closed," Doctor Tan agreed. "Don't worry, once we let the park know, I'm sure they'll wait to pull the ride down until we can get the bats out safely."

"Let's go now," Jay said.

Ebony and Jay wanted to come to Super World with the vets, since they were the ones to find the microbats and the colony.

"What about the babies?" Doctor Bat said kindly. She handed them some more milk solution to take home. "How about we go after you give them their next feed? We have some other work here to do first anyway."

Back home, Ebony put Robyn down on a blanket on the ground in the backyard so she could start getting used to the fresh air. Jay did the same with Batman. The microbats were getting stronger already. Ebony put a rolled blanket down for the bats to climb on. They started crawling around on the blankets, pulling themselves along with their front wing hands in a crawl.

"Look at them go!" Jay said, as Batman

scooted underneath the rolled blanket.

Ebony reached out her hand to Robyn and patted her soft back. The baby snuggled into her gloved hand. Then Robyn took off, hiding under another piece of material. She poked her head out and sniffed the air. Ebony leaned in and she hid behind the blanket again.

"I think she's playing hide-and-seek with me," Ebony said.

Robyn poked her head out again and then hid back behind the blanket when Ebony came closer.

"They really are social, just like the vets said," Jay replied, as Batman scampered onto his outstretched hand.

After the bats had crawled around they hung upside down off the Eco Rangers' hands!

"I wonder if they ever get confused about which way is up," Jay said, tilting his head to one side.

Ebony laughed. "It must be fun being able to hang upside down like that. I think they're ready for bed though."

Ebony and Jay wrapped the babies up in the pouches again. They still needed to be kept warm until their fur grew some more.

Later that afternoon, at the entrance gate to Super World, Doctor Bat and Doctor Tan asked to speak with the theme park manager. The teenage attendant rolled his eyes, picked at a pimple on his face, then rang the office on the park phone.

"Some people are here to see you," he said into the phone in a flat voice. "Um, vets or something they said… mmm, hmm." He held the phone in his hand and looked at Doctor Bat. "Do you have an appointment?" the bored attendant said.

"No, tell the manager it's an emergency," Doctor Bat said.

"They say it's an emergency," he said into the phone, sounding like it was anything but urgent. He hung up and looked at Doctor Bat again. "She'll be here in a few minutes."

Ebony's hands became sweaty as she waited, wondering what the manager would say. She wiped them on the front of her jeans. Then a park cart pulled up in front of them with a screech. The security guard that had caught them out in the demolition zone was driving.

*Oh great*, Ebony thought. *He already has it in for us.* A woman stepped out of the cart and walked through the exit gate and over to them at a brisk pace, followed by the guard. Her lips were pursed tight as she clip-clopped toward them in high heels. She sure didn't look like someone who loved rides, or kids. She peered down her nose at the Eco Rangers, like they had just stood in dog poo.

"And how can I help you?" she said slowly.

Doctor Bat and Doctor Tan each held up their vet cards. They explained they were from the wildlife hospital and that the Eco Rangers had found the microbat colony.

"And that's the emergency I have been called out of my office for?" the manager sneered.

"It could be, for the bats, if we don't rehome them," Doctor Bat said.

"And what exactly were these… children… doing in a restricted area?" the manager said, glaring at the Eco Rangers.

"Yeah, I caught them snooping around earlier today," the security guard said.

The manager glared at him and he clamped his mouth closed.

"The gate was open," Ebony blurted.

"The point is, we're lucky the kids found the bats," Doctor Bat said, calmly. "The animals need to be relocated to a safe place. But it will take time."

"Time?" the manager said, as though she didn't know what the word meant.

"Yes," Doctor Tan said. "It can take a month or more to relocate microbats."

The manager stared straight at Doctor Tan then, who shuffled uncomfortably from foot to foot. "You do realize the new rollercoaster must be completed in time for the summer school break. It's our busiest time. Demolition must begin on schedule."

"Y-yes," Doctor Tan stammered.

"And where are the creatures going to go anyway? Not near my guests."

"Bats are nocturnal," Doctor Tan said.

"So? People will panic if they see bats flying around."

"Nocturnal means they only come out at night, when your guests are gone," Doctor Bat said, rolling her eyes. "We can put up roosting boxes around the park."

"You want to put up what?"

"Roosting boxes. They're small wooden

boxes with a hole at the front that bats like to go into. They're just like a hollow in a tree for them that they'd usually live in."

"You can't do that! They'd look ugly."

"You'd hardly notice they were there. And we wouldn't need many, just a few we can nail up."

*This isn't going well*, Ebony thought.

"Microbats are protected animals," Doctor Bat said. "I'm sure you understand, that it would not be good for the future of this park if you don't have them relocated responsibly."

The smirk on the manager's face faded. Ebony wanted to give Doctor Bat a high five.

"But of course, we wouldn't want anything dreadful to happen to the poor, dear bats," she said, through clenched teeth. "I'll give you three weeks to get them out. Then the ride comes down. And those boxes will have to go somewhere unnoticeable for the guests. Gary!" she yelled.

The security guard tugged on his beard and bared his teeth at the Eco Rangers, like a wolf.

"It's Barry, Ms. Pitts," the guard said.

"Well, Gary Barry, give these… people… an access pass."

"Are you sure? These kids—"

"Are you questioning me?" she snapped. "Give it to them now."

"Okay," he muttered into his beard.

The guard removed a pass from his pocket and handed it to Ebony.

"Not to the kids, you idiot! Give it to the wildlife people."

"We're vets, actually, Ms. Pitts," Doctor Bat said.

The guard gave it to them.

"You can enter the site out of our operating hours only. I don't want the park guests being disturbed. The show must go on, as they say." Ms. Pitts attempted a laugh, which came out more like a hiccup.

"Don't worry, no one will even know we've been here," Doctor Tan said.

"Good! Make sure of it."

The park manager turned on her high heels, made her way back through the entrance terminal, and got back into the cart.

"Step on it, Gary Barry."

Barry quickly ran back to the cart, climbed in, swung it around and rode off. The Eco Rangers and vets let out a big sigh. The bat colony would be saved.

Batman and Robyn were growing bigger every day and they were even starting to have some mealworms (yuck!) in their feeds. Soon they'd be ready to be moved into an enclosure in Ebony's backyard. But although it had seemed they had plenty of time, the three weeks Ms. Pitts had given them for relocation of the microbat colony were already nearly over. It wasn't as easy as just getting the bats out of the tunnel. They had to have somewhere to go first. That meant the roost boxes had to be built before they even tried to relocate them. Plus, they had to care for the babies until they were ready to join their extended family.

Ebony and Jay stepped through the doors on Sunday afternoon, and Judy at the front desk waved the Eco Rangers through, her strawberry-blonde curls bouncing happily.

At least twelve people were working on the roost boxes. *Wow, there are so many people here*, Ebony thought. She had never seen the center so busy. There were pieces of pine wood, shade cloth, nails, hammers and hinges covering the big table everyone was working at.

When they first started a week ago, there was hardly enough wood and other materials they needed to build the boxes, and no one to help. Now look at it. The materials had all been donated from people in their community, and everyone was here to help build them. Ebony smiled. Lots of people did care about the bats. She went over to her own almost-finished box.

She just had to tack on the shade cloth, so the bats had something to climb up to get into the box. She held it tightly across the box and tapped in the last nails to hold the cloth in place. Finally, it was finished.

"Ouch!" Jay yelled, hitting his thumb with the hammer instead of the nail for the umpteenth time.

Ebony turned to see him fumbling with his roost box.

"Can I help?" she asked with a smile.

Jay nodded. He held the box upright while Ebony attached the hinges for the lid of his box. His box was finally finished too. She looked at their handiwork. Their boxes weren't quite as neat as in the picture they had to copy the directions from, especially since they were made of wood scraps they'd found at the recycling plant. But the boxes did have four sides, a hinged roof and some old shade cloth hanging from the bottom as the mesh landing pad for the bats. It had everything a microbat needed.

"Pretty good," Jay said.

Ebony agreed and both were proud to show off their roost boxes to the vets.

"Well done, Eco Rangers," Doctor Bat said. "We almost have enough for the colony now."

"Yes, they're nearly all finished, and then it'll be time to put them up at Super World," Doctor Tan said. "We're running out of nails though, we have so many helpers. Would you mind going down to the hardware store to get us some more, Eco Rangers?"

Jay nodded.

"Sure!" Ebony said, taking the money the vet handed her.

Ebony and Jay dropped their bikes at the front of the hardware store. Inside, they scanned the shelves for the nails.

They crouched at the bottom shelves where they were kept, looking at the various nails.

"What type?" Jay said, looking at the boxes.

"Hmm, let's go with these ones," Ebony said.

Jay picked up a pack of small nails and shook them. Then Ebony heard two familiar voices.

"Shhh!" she said.

Jay held the box still. Ebony peered through the shelves. She could see two sets of feet, one small pair in high heels and one large pair in work boots. Where else had she seen two such mismatching pairs of feet? She peered through the next shelf up. It was Ms. Pitts and Barry, the security guard. But what were they doing here? Ebony peered through the shelf above her. There was arguing as they picked things in the store.

"What about this one?" the security

guard said.

"That's for growing plants, you fool," Ms. Pitts snapped. "We need to exterminate them, not feed them."

Ebony had no idea what they were doing, but it sounded suspicious. She tugged on Jay's sweater sleeve.

"Flying insect spray, insecticide fogger, rat trap," Ms. Pitts said, pointing things out on the shelves that the security guard tossed into the shopping cart. "Bait blocks, bird and animal repellent, outdoor control bomb."

The guard tossed more things into the cart until it was almost full. They either had a big pest problem at the park or they were up to no good!

"That should get rid of the rodents," Barry said, slapping his hands together. "Now we just need a shovel."

They started heading toward the front of the store, toward the aisle the Eco Rangers were hiding in.

"Move back!" Ebony said. "They're coming this way!"

Ebony and Jay sneaked back behind the shelves in the next row as the security guard wheeled the cart up to the checkout. Ms. Pitts clacked behind in her high heels.

"Don't worry 'bout a thing, Ms. Pitts. This plan will work to get rid of 'em," the guard said.

"It had better, Harry," she said.

"It's Barry!"

*What were they trying to get rid of?* Ebony had a horrible feeling it wasn't just rats or insects, with all that gear they'd just bought.

"I think that stuff is for the microbats," she whispered. "Come on, let's go before they see us."

Jay followed but as he turned he dropped the box of nails. The metal pins clattered on the floor.

"Oops!" he said.

Ebony and Jay quickly gathered the nails and ran toward the exit of the hardware store, but at that moment Ms. Pitts spotted them.

"You're those kids—" she began.

Ebony pulled Jay toward the checkout. She dropped their money on the counter and they quickly exited.

❀

Ebony and Jay cycled fast back to the conservation center. They rushed in, the Eco Rangers talking over the top of each other as they tried to tell the vets about the possible plot to kill the microbats.

"Whoa," Doctor Bat laughed. "Slow down and explain it from the start."

Ebony told Doctor Bat exactly what they'd seen and heard.

"I'm sure they're not trying to harm the bats," Doctor Bat said.

"But they bought all that insect spray

and repellents and rat bait and—" Jay said.

"Yes, well, I'm sure it's just for rats, or insects, or something. Anyway, even if it is like you say, I'm sure they're not silly enough to think that would kill the bats," Doctor Bat said.

"It wouldn't?" Jay asked.

"No, bats eat flying insects so they're not going to eat rat poison, and insect sprays would do nothing, except maybe kill off a bit of their food source."

"Oh!" Ebony said, embarrassed. "That's good though."

"Sure is," Jay agreed.

"Now, let's finish off these last roost boxes," Doctor Tan said, "and we'll be ready for the microbat relocation."

6

Ebony and Jay held the roost box still while Doctor Tan tapped in the final nail. It was the last box to go up on the back of the machinery shed at Super World. It was the perfect spot, right opposite the bat colony. Their work was finished, and there were still a few days until the old ride would be pulled down.

"That should make everyone happy," Doctor Bat said. "And by everyone, I mean Ms. Pitts. The boxes are away from the guest areas, and the bats should fly straight out of the tunnel to settle in them."

"Yes, and it's nearly dusk," Doctor Tan said.

"That means it's time for the bat exclusion," Doctor Bat said.

"The what?" Jay said.

"Come and I'll show you," she said.

The Eco Rangers followed the vets to the ride entrance. Doctor Tan pulled out a big piece of netting.

"We'll tape this over the entrance in a funnel shape. That way, when the bats fly out to feed at dusk they won't be able to get back in."

"We don't want them to put themselves back in danger," Doctor Bat added.

"But where will they go?" Jay asked, worried.

"When the bats find they can't return to the ride they'll look for other places to roost. That's where the boxes come in. They'll soon see them as their best new home, and eventually most of them will settle in there, though a few might find other tree hollows or bark to roost under."

The vets stretched the piece of netting across the opening of the ride. Ebony held one side up while Jay held the other. The vets stuck it on using thick gray strips of tape, leaving a gap at the bottom for the bats to fly out. As they layered the tape over the top, Ebony heard a rustling sound.

"Did anyone hear that?" she asked.

"What?" Jay said.

"In the grass over there," she said.

Ebony peered at the bushes. She thought she saw movement.

"There's something there," she insisted.

"It's probably just a skink or some other small animal. The bush gets busy at dusk when the day animals go to bed, and the nocturnal animals start coming out," Doctor Bat said.

"But I'm sure—"

When Ebony looked again there was

nothing there. The bushes were still. Maybe the vets were right, it was just a lizard or something. Ebony concentrated on holding the netting in place. Doctor Tan stuck the last piece of tape on. When Ebony and Jay let go, the netting held.

"Good job, everyone," he said. "In just a few minutes it'll be dark."

"Yes, time to leave them to fly out to catch insects," Doctor Bat said. "Let's go."

Ebony and Jay said goodbye to the bats, hoping they could get the colony safely out of the ride tunnel.

❧

The Eco Rangers rode their bikes straight to Ebony's house after school the next day. Batman and Robyn were big enough to fly around in their own enclosure, so today Ebony and Jay worked hard setting one up for their baby bats. Their part-time home was made from a mesh tent they had borrowed from one of the conservation center volunteers. They'd placed the tent in Ebony's backyard where their furry friends would be able to practice flying and eventually catching insects. Ebony and Jay hung new bats' pouches inside the tent for them to sleep in and set up water and food bowls. Jay's stomach growled noisily as they made their way from the backyard.

"I'm hungry," Jay said.

"Me too, let's have something to eat before we feed Batman and Robyn and introduce them to their new home," Ebony said.

She went inside and asked her mom if they could have some dinner.

"Sure, you go check on the bats. I'm making soup for you, but it's not ready just yet. My Eco Rangers have to keep their strength up!"

Ebony gave her mom a quick hug and went to check on Batman and Robyn. The bats were in their pouches, sleeping.

"We'll need the mealworms," Jay said.

Soon it would be time for the Eco Rangers to hand-feed them some of the mealworms to help the bats grow big and strong.

"Oh right," Ebony said. "I put them in the fridge. The vets said they live longer that way because the cool air puts them into hibernation. I'll be right back."

Ebony ran inside but as she opened the back door she heard a scream. She raced in to see what was wrong.

"Mom!" she cried.

Ebony raced to the kitchen to find her mom holding an open container. Her eyes were wide with fear as she stared into it.

"What's in this?" Mom gasped.

Ebony took the container from her. She laughed when she saw what was inside.

"That's the mealworms for the bats, Mom!"

"Oh, right, of course," she said, breathing out slowly. "They nearly landed in your soup! I'll call you when it's ready."

Back outside, the Eco Rangers took the bats into their new enclosure. Jay put the bats down on the ground and they crawled around, exploring, and then hid behind some branches. Ebony pulled a brown wiggling mealworm out of the container and held it out. Robyn was the first to come out from her hiding spot. She sniffed the air and moved her ears then scrambled toward the worm. She quickly grabbed it and munched her mealworm, her little jaw moving up and down superfast, like she was in fast forward. Then she crawled back to her hiding spot. Jay wiggled another worm near where Batman was hiding. He was shy about coming out and kept poking his head in and out, his little black eyes peering around. Jay moved the worm closer and this time Batman grabbed hold of it.

The bats kept playing hide-and-seek as they gobbled down their worms.

When they were full, Ebony and Jay let their superheroes go. They were so funny, crawling along the mesh in their enclosure. Ebony changed the water in the bowl and Jay cleaned up any mess they had left.

"Why do I always get the dirty jobs?" Jay said.

"I already changed the smelly water," she shot back, with a grin.

"And what about our dinner?" he whined.

"Oh, I forgot. It should be ready now," Ebony said. "Although, I should warn you that you did nearly get mealworm soup instead."

"What?" Jay said.

"Don't worry, I saved you," she laughed.

The next day after school, the Eco Rangers were excited to return to Super World to see how their microbat colony was doing in the new roost boxes. When they got to the

Wild Jungle ride they were shocked to see the netting had come down.

"Oh no!" Jay said, holding the edge of the dangling netting. "How did that happen?"

"Maybe the tape wasn't strong enough," Ebony said. She looked at it closely. "Wait, it's been cut down."

"Let me see," Jay said. He tried to put the net back up, but the pieces wouldn't join. There was a big gap in the middle.

"See? There's a bit missing," Ebony said.

"That's weird," Jay said. "I wonder what happened."

Ebony shrugged. Then she remembered the noise she'd heard and the movement in the bushes when they were putting the net up. Had something, or someone, been waiting until they were gone to pull it down? But who, or what? It didn't make sense.

"Come on! We should check if there are any bats in the roost boxes," Ebony said.

Ebony peered into the first box through the slit at the top, but there was no sign of any bats in there. She tried the next, and the next. They were all empty. There was something lying by the side of the shed though. Ebony picked it up.

"What is it?" Jay asked.

"A can of insect repellent." She shook the can. "It's empty."

"Why would there be insect repellent left outside?" Jay asked.

"Let's check the tunnel," Ebony urged.

She and Jay walked down the tunnel and arrived in the cave where they'd first found the colony. There were small blue blocks lying around.

"What are they?"

"That's rat poison!" Ebony cried. "Don't touch it, Jay!"

And Jay quickly moved his hand away.

Ebony shone her flashlight up on the ceiling. It moved like a wave.

"Oh no! The bats are all back in here," Ebony said.

Then Jay let out a huge yelp. Ebony turned. He was jumping around in a circle and yelling.

"Something's attacking me," he screamed. "Get it off!"

Ebony looked at his foot, held up in the air. It had something attached to it.

"Stop moving!" she said, giggling.

Jay hopped on one spot, a tray dangling from his foot. Ebony bent down and pulled it off Jay's foot with a yank. It was a rat trap. She had seen that kind of glue trap before... In the shopping cart Ms. Pitts and Barry had loaded up with baits and sprays and other awful things.

"This is the work of that Ms. Pitts," Ebony said.

"But why would they be spraying for

insects, and what's with the rat traps?" Jay said, pulling the sticky mess from his foot.

"I don't know, but we need to get the bats out of here before they try something that could really hurt them," Ebony said.

Ebony was tired by the time she got home, and worried about the bat colony. She put the key in the lock and opened the door to her house, when she was met with an ear-piercing scream.

"Help! Help!" her mom was calling.

Ebony raced toward the living room. Had burglars broken into their house? Were they still inside? Ebony felt her stomach twist in knots. Then she saw that her mom was leaning against the wall, her eyes darting back and forth. Two black shapes were flying around the room, zipping past her, over and over again. Ebony stifled a laugh. The baby bats were on the loose!

"What happened, Mom?"

"I-I thought I'd bring them in and feed them for you. It was getting late," her mom stammered. "I was only gone for a minute, to get their food, but by the time I came back they were flying all over the place."

This time Ebony did laugh.

"It's okay, Mom. This is good news."

"It is?"

"Yes, it means they can fly by themselves. And that means they can join their colony soon."

"That's wonderful, darling. But what about now? How do we catch them?" She squealed as Batman and Robyn flew past her once more.

Ebony's mom clapped her hands and stomped her feet noisily, trying to shoo them away. It just made the bats fly faster. Ebony knew she couldn't catch the microbats while they were flying. They had to be still. They could get hurt if she tried to grab them while they were moving.

"Mom, we need to be quiet if we want them to stop flying around, so I can catch them."

Her mom stopped clapping and stomping, and the bats slowed right down.

"What now? They're still flying, just not as fast," her mom said. "Oh, look. They're heading toward the kitchen. Maybe they're hungry."

Ebony watched the bats. They didn't eat human food, or even know what a kitchen was. It couldn't be hunger that was luring them in. She squinted to see where they were. It was dim, with nothing but the street lights shining in through the window. That was it! They were flying away from the bright light of the living room.

"We need to turn all the lights off," Ebony said. "And pull the curtains closed."

"Why on earth would we do that?" Ebony's mom said.

"They're bats, they don't like the light, Mom," Ebony explained. "They are trying to get away from it."

Ebony's mom nodded.

They ran around turning off lights and closing the curtains, so no street light got in. They waited quietly in the dark for a few minutes and then Ebony slowly pulled the curtains apart a little, so they could see. She looked around. The bats had landed in a corner by the couch. Ebony got a piece of baby blanket and scooped the microbats up.

"Aren't they extra cute now they've started to grow fur? They're so much darker and more like real bats too, don't you think?"

"They sure are," Ebony's mom replied.

Ebony noticed they were covered in dust from flying around the house.

"Now, you'll need to be cleaned up a bit," Ebony told the babies.

Ebony washed the bats just as she'd been shown, using baby wipes and some baby shampoo. She groomed them with a dental brush until their dark fur shone it was so smooth.

"What do you think, Batman and Robyn?" Ebony said. She picked up the bats and patted their soft backs. They closed their eyes as they were patted and snuggled into her hand. "You're going to be big and strong enough to join your colony soon!"

The bats shook and wiggled their little noses. They moved their big ears around like they were listening to her. She took the bats back outside to their enclosure and put them back in their pouches. They fell straight to sleep—their adventures in the house must have worn them out. That gave her an idea. The baby bats had shown her a way they could get the rest of their colony out of the ride safely. She couldn't wait to tell Jay her plan.

✗

Ebony and Jay cycled as quickly as they could to Super World again the next afternoon. Ebony was determined her plan to get the bats out would work before Ms. Pitts and her accomplice, Barry, could harm the microbats. Inside his backpack, Jay carried a big flashlight he'd insisted on bringing for extra light, while Ebony got out their passes. She handed Jay his one and raced ahead of him to the Super World entrance.

She scanned her pass at the gate. But instead of the familiar beep before the gate opened, the card reader made a *da doong* sound, and a big red cross came up on the screen.

"My pass isn't working!"

Jay scanned his, but the same thing happened. They went up to the ticket booth. The same pimply attendant was there, biting his fingernails. Ebony explained how their passes weren't working.

The attendant looked up, still biting his nails. "Oh, it's you!"

Just then Ms. Pitts arrived in the park cart. Barry the security guard was driving. They went out the exit gate to meet the Eco Rangers. Something weird was going on.

"What are you kids doing here?" Ms. Pitts snapped.

The Eco Rangers looked at each other. Ebony swallowed hard.

"I know what you kids are up to, but it's too late now," Ms. Pitts said smugly. "The ride is being knocked down. Today!"

"But it's been less than three weeks," Ebony cried. "And the bats are still in there!"

"They'll get hurt," Jay added.

"Exactly!" Ms. Pitts sneered. "I hate bats."

"She has chiroptophobia," Barry said.

"Chiro what?" Jay said.

"It's a fear of bats," he replied.

"And now those horrible flying mice will be destroyed along with the ride," Ms. Pitts said.

"They're not rodents," Jay said. "They have hands on the end of their wings. They're from the hand-wing family, they're—"

"Wait! You think they're rodents?" Ebony said. "You were trying to kill them with those rat traps and insect sprays, right?"

"It didn't work, did it? Anyway, I don't care what they are. You actually thought we'd keep them here in the park? In those ridiculous boxes? I can't have them flying around the park. They're ugly, they've got nasty diseases, they leave a mess, and they smell. Bats are a menace."

"They are not!" Ebony said. "They help the farmers' crops, spreading seeds to help things grow. They eat all the pest insects. Mosquitoes, weevils, and grubs—"

"Enough!" Ms. Pitts yelled. She looked at her watch and turned to the guard.

"Come on, Larry!"

"It's Barry," he said.

"Whatever." She called to the attendant. "Tell the demolition people to bring the bulldozer in now. We need to start pulling down the ride."

"Bulldozer?" Ebony screamed.

"Run along home now, children, the adults have work to do," Ms. Pitts said, laughing.

She went back into the park with Barry close behind.

Ebony's whole body shook. There was no way she was going to let anything happen to the bats. She whispered to Jay. He nodded.

"One, two, three... Eco Rangers!"

They took a run-up and leaped over the turnstile.

"Hey, stop!" the attendant yelled.

The Eco Rangers raced through the entrance.

"Get back here!" Ms. Pitts yelled as they

ran past her.

"To the cart!" Barry yelled.

Barry raced to the park cart and jumped on board. Ms. Pitts climbed in next to him.

"Run!" Ebony yelled to Jay.

# 8

The Eco Rangers ran into the park, toward Candy Land on the way to the Wild Jungle ride. The guard turned the cart sharply, in pursuit. Ebony and Jay ran past a princess carrying a basket of flowers. Jay knocked the basket as he passed, creating an explosion of petals.

"Sorry!" Ebony yelled and kept running.

The princess screamed and bent to collect them, just as the cart flew past her, knocking the whole basket out of her hands. She screamed even louder. As they were getting closer to Candy Land, the cart started closing in on them. Ebony saw a side path and raced down it, Jay following.

Ebony looked over her shoulder. The cart was even closer now. How were they ever going to outrun them? Up ahead there was a hotdog stand. The hotdog vendor was loading sausages into buns for waiting customers. Another man was squeezing sauce on his hotdog. If they could just make it through the tight gap between the people who were in line and the stand they might get away. The cart could never squeeze through there.

"Look out!" Ebony squealed as she ran. She and Jay weaved between the hotdog stand and the customers. The cart zoomed through after them, plowing into the hotdog stand, sending hotdogs flying. Hungry customers scattered like seagulls. A man holding a sauce bottle squeezed it in fright, squirting himself in the eye with it.

Ebony and Jay reached Fairytale Castle

and ran through it as fast as they could. The cart zoomed around Fairytale Castle, trying to cut them off. The Eco Rangers ran, the cart following close behind.

"Where now?" Jay puffed.

Ebony scanned the attractions nearby. "The ball pit!"

They ran toward it, shot past the stunned ride operator, and disappeared inside the pit. It was filled with small, squishy colored balls. Ebony and Jay squelched through them. Meanwhile, the cart screeched to a stop. Ms. Pitts and Barry jumped off, running inside after them. Ebony and Jay got to the other end of the pit and climbed out.

"They're getting away!" Ms. Pitts screeched.

She stumbled into the pit after the Eco Rangers, and disappeared in the pile of squishy balls, with just her legs poking out.

"Get me out of here!" she yelled.

Barry came stumbling after her and tried to pull her out. He kept slipping on the balls and fell on top of Ms. Pitts. She shoved him off. They rolled to the side and finally pulled themselves out.

Out of the pit, the Eco Rangers sprinted past two more rides. Jay stopped, his hands on his knees, panting hard. Ebony took a moment to get her breath back too. As she inhaled, she noticed the entrance to an underground tunnel which was leading to the Haunted House ride.

"In there," she said, pointing to it.

"No way!" Jay said, his legs starting to shake just at the thought.

"Come on! It's the only way to lose them," Ebony said, getting her breath back.

She grabbed Jay by the arm and dragged him inside. They ran and ran through the dark tunnel until they reached the entrance of the Haunted House. They disappeared into it and made their way through the dark rooms, ghouls lunging for them. Jay yelped and grabbed Ebony's arm tightly when cobweb spray splattered their faces. Even Ebony was nervous going through it.

They made it through to the end, then ran across the stage of the Rock Lobster kid concert and darted across the bumper cars, dodging the sliding carts as they went, left and right. Ebony glanced over her shoulder. Ms. Pitts and Barry were nowhere to be seen. The Eco Rangers had outrun them.

Finally, they reached the pathway leading to the Wild Jungle ride. Ebony and Jay reached the gate, still with no sign of Ms. Pitts and Barry. By now the two friends were nearly out of breath. They were almost there though. Ebony pulled her phone out of her pocket.

"I need to alert the vets," she puffed. "Hopefully we can hold the demolition off till then." She went to call them, but the screen was black. "Oh no!"

"What is it?" Jay said.

"My battery's flat."

"Now what?" Jay said.

Ebony shook her head. She didn't know how the Eco Rangers were going to stop a gigantic bulldozer and save the bats. But there had to be a way. There just had to.

The Eco Rangers raced over to the ride entrance. There was no sign of the bulldozer yet. They crept into the darkness. Jay pulled the big, heavy flashlight out of his backpack and shone it on the tracks. They stumbled along the tracks, until they reached the bat colony.

"Now what?" Jay said. "How are we going to get them out?"

"When Batman and Robyn were flying around the house, it was because it was too bright and noisy. So, if we can create a lot of sound and light, that should send them out of the ride immediately."

"I can stamp my feet and clap pretty loudly. And I've got this," Jay said, shining his flashlight in Ebony's eyes.

She put her hand over it to shield her eyes. "That's great, but some light and a bit of stomping isn't going to be enough to send out a whole colony."

Jay scratched his head. "What are we going to do then?"

Ebony looked around.

"We need to get this ride going," she declared.

"Bats can't sit on a ride," Jay cried.

"No, but there's always lots of noise and light when you go on a ride. We just have to switch it back on," Ebony said.

"Then they might fly out of the tunnel!" Jay agreed.

"Yes, and remember how Batman and Robyn cling together all the time?"

"Oh yeah, if one bat goes they'll all

follow each other."

"Just like one big happy family," Ebony grinned.

✖

Now they had a plan, the Eco Rangers checked the tracks, the empty vehicles and even the lockers that were for rider hats and bags. They couldn't find a switch for the ride anywhere. Then Ebony noticed a curtained-off area. She went over and pulled back the dusty material. It revealed a glass control booth for the ride. At that moment, she heard a growing rumbling in the distance. She looked at Jay. There was a flash of light. Then it was gone again.

"Is that a storm coming?" she asked.

"I'll go check," Jay said, taking the flashlight.

"Okay! I'll see if I can get the ride working," Ebony said.

Jay ran off down the tunnel. Ebony

opened the door to the control booth. It squeaked as she pushed it open. She stepped inside and felt around in the dark until she found a light switch. She pressed it down. The control box lit up. The power was still working. It smelled musty, and cobwebs and dust coated everything. She wiped the control panel with the back of her sleeve. There was a bank of buttons and switches. She didn't know what they were all for, but she needed to find which ones turned on the lights and music. There were two big orange buttons and some silver switches. She pressed the first button. Nothing happened. She pressed the other one. Still nothing.

Jay came running back up the tunnel.

"Bad news," he said, panting. "It's not a storm."

"Isn't that good news?" Ebony said.

"It's the bulldozer. And it's coming this way."

"Oh no! We have to get the bats out. Fast!" Ebony said.

Ebony tried the buttons again. Still nothing. Frustrated, she pressed them both at once. There was a loud metallic screeching sound.

"It's working!" she cried.

Jay waved his hands in the air.

"Stop! The vehicles are moving!" he yelled.

Ebony looked over. The ride vehicles were moving along the tracks. *Oops!* She released the buttons and the vehicles stopped moving. This time she looked at the silver switches. She pressed the first one down. All the lights for the ride came on.

"Yes!" Ebony cried.

Swirling lights shone on the blue painted floor, making it look like a river. Round spotlights shone on the fake hippo and crocodile, and the carriage lights beamed brightly, illuminating the tunnel.

The Wild Jungle ride was transformed into a rainforest again, except this time it was with real bats hanging from the ceiling!

The microbats slowly started unfolding their wings. It was working! Ebony pressed down the other switch. This time the ride soundtrack began with the dull sound of thumping drums and jungle music. She turned a dial above it. The music got louder.

The bats all flew from the ceiling, and they were moving in a huge cloud of wings and furry bodies, exactly where they wanted them to—toward the exit.

9

The Eco Rangers followed the bats out
of the ride entrance. By now the sky was
twilight blue. Ebony could see the yellow
body of the bulldozer against the darkening
sky. It was heading straight toward the ride
entrance. The jaws of the scoop lowered.
Ms. Pitts and Barry were standing in front
of it, directing the driver to line it up right
in front of the tunnel opening. Ebony felt
her tummy churn. The ride was about to
be pulled down with the bats still inside.

Suddenly a cloud of microbats flew out,
straight into their path. Ms. Pitts let out a

blood-curdling scream as the tiny bats flew toward her.

"Get them off me!" she screamed. "I HATE, I HATE, I HATE BATS!"

"Shoo! Shoo!" the guard said. He waved his arms in the air above him.

Ms. Pitts ran away, as fast as she could in high heels, which wasn't very fast. She tripped on a tuft of grass and face-planted on the ground. Barry turned and ran after her—running straight into the front of a fake tree. He hit his head on it and fell backward onto the ground.

The bulldozer rolled forward. There were still bats in the tunnel. Ebony waved her hands to stop it. Jay jumped up and down, his arms above his head. The driver rubbed his eyes and looked at them again, like he'd been dreaming. He hit the brakes hard, the bulldozer's caterpillar tracks spinning and smoking as the huge vehicle screeched to a stop. The driver pulled open the cab door and stepped out. He was as wide as he was tall, with bulging biceps. He stormed toward the Eco Rangers. Ebony gulped.

"Now might be a good time to run," Jay stammered.

But it was too late for that.

"What are you kids doing here? You could have got yourselves hurt!" the driver growled.

"There are microbats living in here," Ebony said. "We had to get them out before their home was destroyed." The Eco Rangers pointed to the bats that were flying around at the ride entrance.

The driver frowned then leaned forward. "Is... is that the jungle I can hear?"

"We used the ride noises to try and get them out."

"What are those flashing lights? Are those bats having a party in there?"

Ebony and Jay laughed. "No, they don't like the light either. It's the only way we could attempt to rescue them out in time."

"Hmm, it sure seems like you kids know what you're doing. Anything I can do to help get the critters out safe and sound?" the driver said kindly.

Ebony looked over her shoulder. Ms. Pitts brushed down her skirt. Her hair was a crow's nest, and one heel had broken off her shoe. She limped toward them, pointing an angry finger at the Eco Rangers. Barry sat upright against the tree, shaking his head, looking disoriented.

"We could use a little help with them," Ebony said, pointing to Barry and Ms. Pitts. "We need more time for all the bats to fly out."

"Leave it to me," the driver said with a wink.

He turned and walked straight up to Ms. Pitts. She puffed and panted, her bright red cheeks smeared with dirt. Her chest heaved with fury.

"Get that bulldozer moving right now or I'll—"

The driver crossed his big arms across his broad chest. "Not till all the bats are out, Ma'am."

She turned angrily on the kids. "Why you little… Harry Larry, do something."

"What?" the dazed guard said.

"Get up, you idiot!" she screamed.

He was getting to his feet when the bulldozer driver stepped up to him, his chest in Barry's face.

"Are you trying to stop these bats from getting out safely?" he growled.

"What? Where am I?" Barry said, confused after knocking his head on the tree.

"You're fired!" Ms. Pitts screamed at him.

She looked around furiously, then spied the now empty bulldozer cabin. She made a run for it.

"Hey!" Ebony screamed.

The Eco Rangers chased after her but by the time they reached the cabin, Ms. Pitts had already started the engine. Ebony tried to wrench open the cabin door, but it was no use. Ms. Pitts had locked herself inside. Ebony banged on the window, but the park manager ignored her.

The bulldozer started moving. Jay pulled Ebony back safely out of the way. They watched helplessly as the huge vehicle rolled straight toward the ride. There were still bats flying out. They needed more time for them to all wake and fly out safely.

"We have to stop her!" Ebony cried. "There are still some bats further inside."

Just as the words left her mouth, the edge of the ride opening came crashing down as the dozer rammed into it. Great chunks of concrete rained down on the hood as Ms. Pitts reversed the vehicle.

"We can't let her destroy the main cave until every bat is safely out," Ebony yelled.

She looked around for something, anything that could help them. She saw the tree the security guard had knocked into. It was on a lean from the impact. If only she was strong enough to pull it out. She turned to the big, muscly dozer driver. If anyone could pull that tree out, he could. Ebony raced over to him and asked for his help. He nodded and in three gigantic strides he was at the fake tree. Ms. Pitts revved the engine hard, crunching the gears into drive.

"She's going to knock the whole ride down," Jay yelled.

"Quick!" Ebony begged the driver.

He bent his legs in front of the tree and hugged it firmly. He heaved, and the tree lifted out of the ground a little. He heaved again. It moved some more but it wasn't enough. "We're going to have to pull it down the rest of the way," he yelled.

He put his huge hands against the tree and leaned on it with all his weight.

Ebony and Jay ran over and helped push. The tree came down with a huge thump. The three of them dragged the tree over to the ride. Ms. Pitts was already accelerating again toward the ride. They laid the tree down in front of the entrance. It was too late by the time she saw it. The dozer slammed into the front of it and Ms. Pitts was thrown back in her seat. The engine ran with the dozer's caterpillar tracks spinning uselessly.

10

At that moment, a white van with weird
antennas on the top came roaring toward
them. It skidded to a stop in front of them,
coating them all in a fine layer of road dirt.
Two men quickly stepped out of the van,
followed by a blonde woman. She had a
microphone in her hand. The two men
took out a huge camera from the trunk and
were holding it in front of her.

"I'm Lucy from Coast Network TV
and I'm talking to the manager of Super
World theme park about their exciting new
development." She gestured to the dozer,

bouncing her curls with her hand. "And it looks like we're just in time to see the demolition take place. You're seeing this live, guys!"

Lucy rapped on the cabin window. The dishevelled Ms. Pitts bolted upright to come face to face with the smiling reporter. Hardly realising what was happening, Ms. Pitts opened the cabin. The reporter stuck a big microphone in Ms. Pitts' dust-streaked face. Ebony and Jay looked at each other and giggled. Ms. Pitts turned white.

"What's happening?" she said through clenched teeth.

"You did call us out to film the demolition as it happened, did you not? You're live on the air now, Mrs. ah—"

"Pitts. Ms. Pitts," she said as she opened the cabin and stepped out. She quickly pressed down her unruly hair and tried to stand evenly on her broken heel, putting on one of her fake smiles.

"So, Ms. Pitts, what can you tell us about the demolition that's happening here?"

"Yes, yes," she said, composing herself. "We at Super World are very excited to be making way for the very, ah, thrilling new ride. The Nightmare Flyer. It, um, will be the biggest rollercoaster for a theme park ever." She laughed nervously, still trying to flatten down her hair.

"Well, that sounds thrilling indeed," Lucy said. She turned and spotted Ebony and Jay standing there, still giggling. She headed straight toward them.

"I see we have two keen young theme park-goers with us today."

"No, not them. Don't talk to those children!" Ms. Pitts yelled.

The reporter ignored her and stepped up to the Eco Rangers.

"What are your names?" Lucy said, shoving the microphone in their faces. Jay looked terrified, but Ebony winked at him.

She had an idea.

"I'm J-J-Jay," he said.

"And I'm Ebony," she replied.

"Well, Jay and Ebony, are you excited about the new ride?"

"Y-y-yes," Jay said.

"We sure are," Ebony said. "I love thrill rides, especially now the park has dedicated the new Nightmare Flyer to the microbats that are being rescued."

Jay nodded like a stunned robot.

"We've what?" Ms. Pitts cried.

Lucy turned her back to Ms. Pitts. "Tell us more, Ebony," she said.

"When the park found the microbats living inside the old ride, they organized to get them out safely before the new ride would be built. There will even be a donation box where guests can help save these special animals. Isn't that right, Ms. Pitts?"

Ms. Pitts' face had turned from white

to bright red. She was clutching at the top button of her shirt like it was choking her.

"How wonderful," Lucy said, pointing the microphone back in Ms. Pitts' face.

"Ha, yes," Ms. Pitts said, looking like she was about to be sick.

"Ms. Pitts didn't realize there were still microbats inside the ride," Ebony continued. "She stopped the bulldozer just in time, so they could all get out safely."

"That's great! It was lovely to meet you kids."

"Thanks, we're the Eco Rangers," Ebony and Jay said, winking at each other. Jay sounded a little braver.

"Eco Rangers?" she said. "That's catchy, I like it. And what is it you do, Eco Rangers?"

"We help the local conservation center rescue and care for injured and sick wildlife."

"Well, isn't that awesome, everyone? It's so refreshing to see our young people caring about animals. There you have it, folks. Not only is a super thrill ride coming soon, The Nightmare Flyer, but the theme park is doing its bit to help our native wildlife. This is Lucy from Coast Network TV, signing out, live from Super World."

Lucy made a cross sign to end the filming. The cameraman switched off the video.

"Brilliant! That went very well, don't you think?" Lucy said, turning to Ms. Pitts.

At that moment, the rest of the microbats flew out, straight toward Ms. Pitts. She stared at the incoming bats with wide-eyed horror then half limped, half ran away from them, waving her hands in the air and screaming.

"She's a very busy lady," Lucy chuckled nervously.

"Eco Rangers, it would be great to chat to you some more about your wonderful work. Maybe we can set up an interview?"

"We'd love that, wouldn't we, Jay?"

Ebony nudged Jay who was still trying

to overcome stage fright. He nodded his head in agreement.

Lucy shook their hands and said goodbye. Ebony grinned, knowing the microbats were now safe forever.

Ebony and Jay were famous after their live TV appearance and everyone at school was now calling them the Eco Rangers. Mostly, everyone asked questions to Ebony, since Jay had got a serious case of stage fright on camera. He was happy to sign autographs for some of the younger kids at school though. The best thing about it was that everyone knew the bats were there to stay at Super World.

The Eco Rangers had been checking the roost boxes to see how the colony was doing every day after school. They had settled in to their new homes well. After starring on the news, they even had plenty of volunteers helping them out with moving the boxes into the nearby bushland, where they'd be safe forever.

A few days later it was time to get everything ready to release the microbats. The vets were about to do their last health check, and then Batman and Robyn would be free to join their bat family in the colony.

"Right, let's see how our little superheroes are going," Doctor Bat said as he walked out to the enclosure. "Hmm, they're flying well. Catching insects on their wings."

"They're eating. Drinking from their water bowl too," Doctor Tan added.

Doctor Bat then picked one bat up at a time and looked them over. "Clean fur. Strong wings. Fat little tummies," she said. She put them carefully back in their warm pouches, hanging inside the tent. "Yes, I think they are indeed two little healthy heroes. We can return them to their colony tonight!"

Word had spread that it was time for the baby bats to be returned home. A huge crowd gathered to see Batman and Robyn being released. Ebony was glad Ms. Pitts and Barry were nowhere to be seen. Ebony held Robyn in her hand and Jay held Batman in his.

"It's time to join your bat family," Ebony said. "It's not the same as your bat cave, but I think you'll make good superheroes here, too!"

Batman moved his ears around and Robyn wriggled in Ebony's hand. She looked at Jay. He was wiping his eye behind his glasses.

"Are you crying?" she said.

"Huh? Of course not. I just… have some grit in my eye."

"Then why are your glasses fogged up?" Ebony grinned.

"Stop it!" he said. "Anyway, admit it, you'll miss them too."

"True," Ebony agreed.

She looked proudly at the cute little bats they had hand-reared, and Jay gave Batman one last pat goodbye on his soft back. The babies had been part of their family over the past few weeks. It was sad to see them go. Ebony placed Robyn in a roost box, and Jay put Batman next to her, the two bats huddling together in their new home.

At that moment, a microbat flew out of one of the other roost boxes and circled around Ebony.

"What's this bat doing? It's not time for catching insects yet."

The bat made a *tick-tick* sound then it glided toward the roost box Batman and Robyn were in. It disappeared inside the box. Ebony and Jay looked at each other, both thinking the same thing.

"I think we've found Batman and Robyn's mom," Jay said.

"Yes, it looks like she's located her babies," Doctor Tan agreed.

Ebony peeked inside the roost box. Batman and Robyn were huddled in next to their mom.

"Well done, Eco Rangers," Doctor Bat said.

She was interrupted when her phone rang. The vet answered it, and her smile darkened into a frown. "Okay, thank you. We'll be right there."

"What is it?" Ebony asked.

"There's a bushfire that's broken out in bushland on the western coast. Looks like we might have some wildlife that have been caught up in it."

"Oh no!" Ebony said.

"Eco Rangers, we need you on standby

in case we have some animals that need extra care."

Ebony and Jay took one look at each other, and bumped fists.

"Eco Rangers to the rescue!"

# HERE IS A SPECIAL INTERVIEW WITH THE ECO RANGERS. READ ALONG!

## HOW DID YOU FIRST BECOME THE ECO RANGERS?

**Ebony:** One day we were at the beach when we found a pelican covered in oil. It was really sick so we took it to the wildlife hospital.

**Jay:** The vets, Doctor Bat and Doctor Tan, asked us to help clean it up and look after it. On that day, they called us the Eco Rangers for the first time and the name stuck. We've been helping look after wildlife ever since.

## WHAT DO YOU LIKE ABOUT BEING ECO RANGERS?

**Jay:** Solving mysteries and feeding the animals. That's heaps of fun!

**Ebony:** I like getting to know the animals. Some of them are really funny, or cheeky, or cute.

## WHAT'S THE HARDEST THING ABOUT BEING AN ECO RANGER?

**Ebony:** Having to say goodbye when the animals are better and we release them back into the wild.

**Jay:** That's definitely the worst bit. Oh, and cleaning up their… you know, mess!

## HOW DO YOU KNOW HOW TO LOOK AFTER THE ANIMALS?

**Ebony:** We didn't know much at first. But the vets taught us how to care for them and we check in with them all the time. They do all the medical stuff, we help feed the animals and give them somewhere to stay.

**Jay:** Every animal is different too. They have different food, shelter and reasons they need our help.

## WHAT WOULD YOU SAY TO ANYONE WHO FINDS WILDLIFE NEEDING HELP?

**Jay:** Contact your local wildlife hospital right away so they can come help.

**Ebony:** Yeah, that way you can become an Eco Ranger yourself!

# ABOUT THE AUTHOR

**Candice Lemon-Scott** loves wildlife and animals and has always been surrounded by a range of pets throughout her life, including dogs, cats, rabbits, fish, birds (including a duck), and various lizards. She was first moved to write this series after helping with a couple of koala rescues from her own backyard. She continues to be inspired by her own children, Krystalin and Aliena, who love and care for nature and wildlife.

A trained wildlife carer, Candice enjoys writing about the adventures of the young Eco Rangers, Ebony and Jay. Her quirky style, fast-paced narratives and originality appeal to young readers in particular.

Following several years working in the media, Candice now writes for children. This is her second book series.